Miss Irwin

Allen Say

SCHOLASTIC PRESS · NEW YORK

AUTHOR'S NOTE

The teachers I loved and admired are figures of light in my memory. Miss Irwin is especially luminous. She was my daughter's kindergarten teacher. The children's words and drawings and dancing made her blush with excitement. And by trying to keep her blushing, the children learned the astonishment of discovering. I hope she will forgive me for casting her as a forgetful grandmother in this story – it's an attempt to capture her light before all is forgotten.

Allen Say

All rights reserved. Published by Scholastic Press, an imprint of Scholastic Inc., *Publishers since 1920*. SCHOLASTIC, SCHOLASTIC PRESS, and associated logos are trademarks and/or registered trademarks of Scholastic Inc.

The publisher does not have any control over and does not assume any responsibility for author or third-party websites or their content.

Library of Congress Cataloging-in-Publication Data available
ISBN 978-1-338-30040-6

10 9 8 7 6 5 4 3 2 1   23 24 25 26 27
Printed in China   38
First edition, April 2023

The type was set in Century Schoolbook.
The illustrations were created using oil paint on cardboards.
Book design by Charles Kreloff and David Saylor

For Yuriko
and
Margaret Eisenstadt

On his way home, a boy stops by a small house.

"Grandma!" he calls from the front steps. "Your door is open!"

"I'm watering her roses, honey," his mother answers from the backyard. "The kitty is out . . . Keep Grandma company."

"Okay, Mom," he calls back, and goes inside.

"Oh, how delightful!" a woman exclaims. "Just in time for tea, my dear."

The boy puts his backpack down and notices on the shelf a white box he hasn't seen before.

He takes it to the kitchen.

"What's in this box, Grandma?"

"Oh, my dear Willie!" the old woman cries. "Where in the world have you been?"

"I'm Andy, Grandma . . ."

Grandma stares.

Andy looks at her and smiles. He remembers what Mom and Dad told him about Grandma.

"My dear boy, I am not your grandmother."

"What do you mean? Who are you, then?"

"Why, I had you in kindergarten . . . I am Miss Irwin."

"I'm in second grade, Grand . . . I mean, Miss . . ."

"You don't say! . . . How you have grown!"

"Uh, what's in this box, Miss Irwin?"

"The box . . . oh yes, the box . . ." Grandma trails off, then smiles brightly. "Goodness gracious, I thought I had lost it for good . . . Oh, I'm so happy you found it."

"Such a darling little nest, so perfect . . ."

"What kind of nest, Grandma . . . I mean, Miss Irwin? Where did you get it?"

"Hmmm . . . why, it's the hummingbird nest you made for me."

"What? I made it? How?"

Gently, Grandma puts the nest in her hand.

"See all the little twigs and bits of cotton glued together . . . on a wooden chopstick . . . so clever . . . so real."

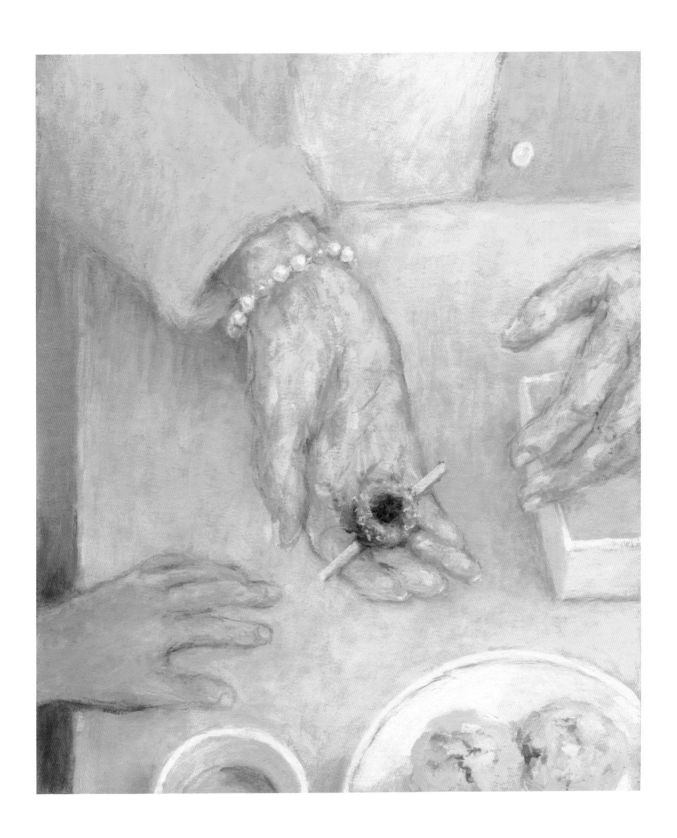

"You stared out the window and made cutout birds all
day . . ." Grandma speaks slowly, with waving hands.

"Just gazing out the window . . . so still . . . so quiet . . .
watching the birds."

"We marched to the plum tree . . ."

"And we looked and waited . . . No one said a word!"

"What were we watching? Where was I?"

"Why, the bird feeder I put on the plum tree, and you followed us . . . My dear . . ." Grandmother's eyes open wide. "You saw the shining ruby neck and the body of green satin . . ." She takes a long breath. "A boy hummingbird . . . Jenny named it Sparkles . . . So clever . . ."

"Oh, and nectar for the little angels . . . A third of a cup of sugar and . . ." Grandma's words fade.

"Water?"

Grandma's lips move. "Ah . . . one and a half cups of hot water, wasn't it? And oh, the book . . . the book! It had so many beautiful pictures of birds . . . You looked and looked . . ."

"Such lovely pictures, so sweet . . . I read about the mother hummingbirds weaving their nests with spider silk . . . then you disappeared at nap time."

"I was just looking, Miss Irwin."

"So you were . . . I knew you were looking for bird nests, remember, yes remember . . . Not to touch any bird nests, ever . . . I think you gave me a nod . . . or perhaps I only wished you did."

"Do you have a book like that now?"

She sips her tea and puts the cup down.

"Why, I gave it to you . . . on my last day . . . Oh, dear . . . you took it and disappeared . . . I was out the gate . . . You came running and gave me a paper bag . . ."

"You opened your mouth . . . I waited . . . but you turned and ran away . . . This precious nest was in the bag."

"Umm . . . I'm glad I gave it to you, Miss Irwin."

"Thank you, darling Willie . . . Wouldn't it be lovely to make nectar again?"

"I'll ask Mom to get us a feeder!"

"I have plenty of sugar . . ."

"A third of a cup, and one and a half cups of hot water!"

"Excellent!"

"It'll be fun to feed the hummingbirds together, Gran . . ."

Grandmother takes his hand. "Nothing would make me happier, Andy."

He smiles. "Let's tell Mom!"

Opening the back door for Grandma, Andy whispers to himself, "I'm going to make her my own nest."